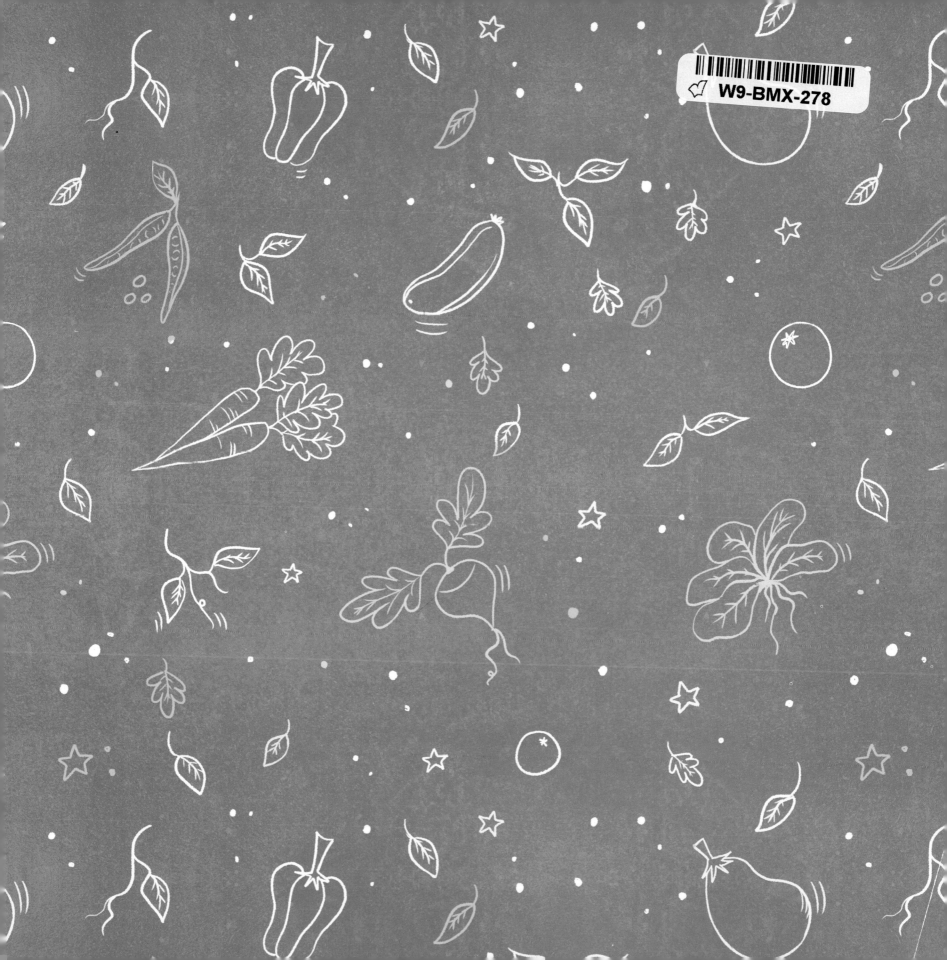

RODALE KiDS
RODALEKIDS.COM

Dedicated to my real-life Bloomers, Cassie, Alex, Sophia, and Mac, the inspiration for Lilly, Big Red, Rosey Posey, and Bud Inski.
Thank you all for providing me with endless fodder for my stories. Thank you, Mom, for teaching me how to garden and thank you,
Dad, for affording me the opportunity to grow up on the vast Adventureland known as Misty Hill Farms. Lucky me.
- C.W.

For budding green thumbs everywhere, that their hearts and minds may grow
as magnificently as their gardens.
- C.B.C.

To my amazing husband and family for supporting and believing in me on this beautiful journey.
Much love and thanks to everyone who follows my books and illustrations.
- K.L.

An imprint of Rodale Books
733 Third Avenue
New York, NY 10017
Visit us online at rodalekids.com

Text © 2018 by Cynthia Wylie and Courtney Carbone

Illustrations © 2018 by Katya Longhi

Rodale Kids books may be purchased for business or promotional use or for special sales.
For information, please e-mail: RodaleKids@Rodale.com

Printed in China

Manufactured by RRD Asia 201709

Design by Christina Gaugler and Ariana Abud

Library of Congress Cataloging-in-Publication Data is on-file with the publisher.

ISBN 978-1-63565-069-3 hardcover

Distributed to the trade by Macmillan

10 9 8 7 6 5 4 3 2 1 hardcover

Bloomers Island

The Great
Garden Party

CYNTHIA WYLIE and **COURTNEY CARBONE**

Illustrated by **KATYA LONGHI**

RODALE
KiDS

A long time ago, a magical island formed where natural things came to life. Plants, trees, and flowers learned to move in order to find what they needed: better soil, more water, and brighter sunlight. They learned to talk, laugh, and make friends. They also learned how to read and tell stories. These curious creatures became known as Bloomers.

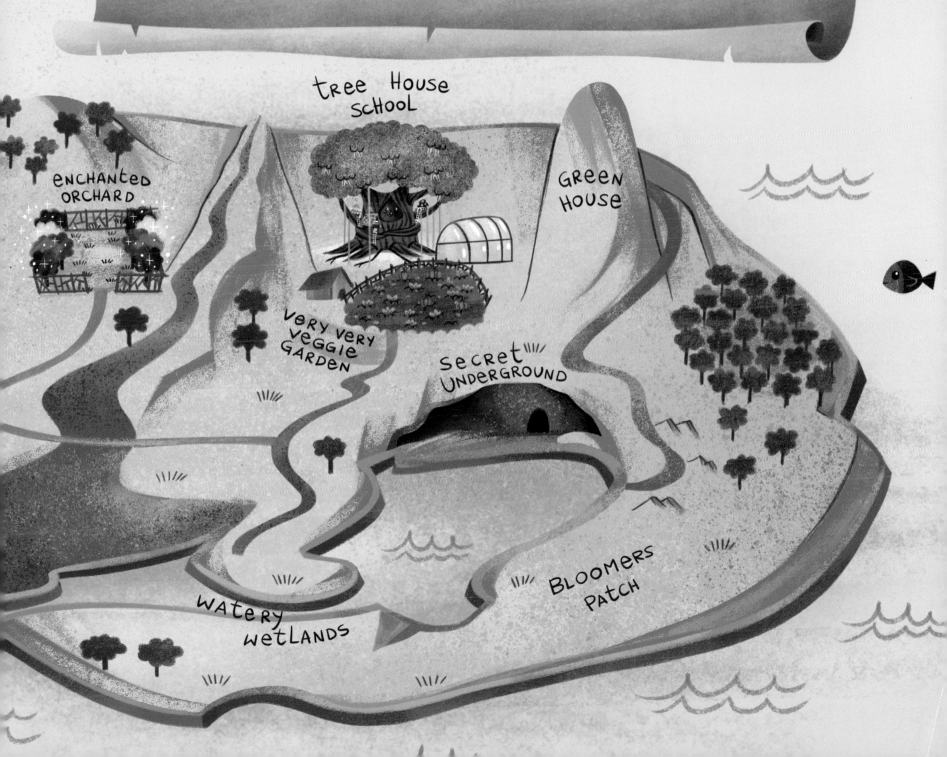

tree House School

enchanted ORCHARD

GREEN House

Very Very Veggie GARDEN

Secret UNDERGROUND

BLOOMERS PATCH

WATERY WETLANDS

It was the first day of school on Bloomers Island. When the students first arrived at their new boarding school, however, they were surprised to see that it was all the way up in a tree!

"Welcome to the Tree House School, Bloomers!" said the headmaster. "My name is **Professor Sage**, and this is **Mr. Banyan**."

He was pointing to the wise old tree holding the school in his arms.

A small green bud stepped forward from behind the headmaster.

"I'm **Bud Inski**!" he said. "I already live here, so I can show you around."

"Thanks, Bud!" said a friendly red and orange flower. "I'm **Lilly**."

"I'm **Rosey Posey**," said the pink flower beside her.

"My name's **Violet**," said a bright purple flower, "and this is my friend **Daisy**." The white flower next to her smiled.

"I'm **Big Red**," said a tall redwood sapling.

"**Pete Moss** here!" said the Bloomer to his right.

"And I'm **Basil**!" a leafy Bloomer added.

"Welcome, everyone," said Professor Sage. "On Bloomers Island, growing crops for food is our way of life. Have any of you ever helped your families garden at home?"

A few hands shot up into the air.

"Great!" Professor Sage continued. "Please follow me."

Professor Sage led the Bloomers into a large garden next to the school. It was full of all kinds of fruits and vegetables. The students' mouths watered. The crops looked so plump and juicy!

"This is the Very Very Veggie Garden," the professor said. "Here, we grow our own food. We tend the garden, and in return, it provides us with everything we need to stay happy and healthy."

"The first thing you will learn in my class is how to garden and grow your own food," Professor Sage said.

The students looked worried. They didn't know anything about gardening!

"What's wrong?" the professor asked.

"To be honest," said Rosey Posey slowly. "Gardening sounds like a lot of work."

"I'm with her," said Basil. "And I don't like getting dirty."

Professor Sage smiled. He had an idea that would change their minds.

The next day, the Bloomers woke with the morning sun. They climbed out of their flowerbeds, got ready, and went down to school.

"So, today, instead of reading and writing about gardening, we are going to have a big surprise!" Professor Sage said.

Everyone cheered.

Professor Sage led the students downstairs toward the Very Very Veggie Garden. When they got to the bottom, the Bloomers saw that the garden was completely transformed from the day before!

"Welcome to the great garden party!" Professor Sage announced.

There were tables full of honey cakes and lanterns with twinkling firefly lights. Everything was covered in colorful streamers and balloons.

The students chattered excitedly. Professor Sage picked up a blade of grass and whistled loudly to get their attention. Everyone looked up.

"We will now have a series of contests, beginning with a scavenger hunt for seeds," he said.

Bud handed out a list of seeds they needed to find in the garden.

The Bloomers formed teams of two:
Violet and Big Red, Rosey Posey and Basil,
Lilly and Bud, and Daisy and Pete Moss.

"Ready, set, GO!" Professor Sage shouted.

The Bloomers collected seeds as fast as they could. Daisy was so fast she made it all the way around the garden before the other teams even had their first seed!

Seed list

- Corn
- pumpkin
- artichoke
- tomato
- pepper
- eggplant
- carrot
- spinach
- sesame
- basil
- sage
- celery
- radish

The next part of the race was a watering can balloon toss. As each balloon was caught, it burst open and the water inside filled up the watering can. Basil had excellent aim, and Rosey Posey loved catching the balloons—especially the pink ones, because they were her favorite color!

The contest continued with a game to see who could dig holes the fastest. Big Red was so strong that he easily took the lead. (But being the kind-hearted tree he was, he then went on to help the others!)

Professor Sage was impressed with his students' progress.

"Now that you have seeds, water, and holes ready for planting, we will move on to the final challenge: Whoever plants and waters all their seeds first wins!"

The students sprang into action. Each team had a different strategy, but Lilly and Bud created a fast and efficient system. They won the final challenge in no time!

Everyone cheered.

"I'm so proud of all of you," Professor Sage said with a smile. "You used many skills and learned the value of teamwork. You are all one step closer to becoming expert gardeners."

The Bloomers looked at each other, surprised. They had been having so much fun that they did not realize they were learning how to garden! Professor Sage's surprise had been a great success.

Professor Sage said, "And remember Bloomers, everything is always more fun when it's a party. Now, let's eat honey cake!"

From then on, the Bloomers were excited about gardening!

"See?" Professor Sage told them. "Learning about anything can be fun if you have an open mind."

"So, what now, Professor?" Violet asked, eagerly.

"Next we will learn about growing different kinds of vegetables," Professor Sage replied. "We will have a class contest to see who can grow the biggest and best one!"

The students couldn't wait to get started. They all talked excitedly about which vegetable they wanted to grow. Professor Sage knew that it was only just the beginning of his Bloomers' gardening adventures.

Meanwhile, overwhelmed with happiness and pride,
Mr. Banyan hugged his tree house just a little bit tighter.

School

MEET THE

Basil

Basil is a friend to almost everyone on Bloomers Island. He has good manners and always tries to remember to say, "please" and "thank you."

Bud Inski

Bud loves to read and figure stuff out. Growing up with Professor Sage, he's read almost every book in the library. If anyone needs a fact or statistic to support an argument, they can count on Bud to provide it.

Big Red

Big Red is the peacemaker among the Bloomers. He is always cool, calm, and collected. He's the first to pitch in to help and look out for the little plant, which is just about everyone compared to him.

Daisy

Daisy's a musician who has mastered all kinds of instruments, but her favorite is the fiddle-headed fern. She is shy and doesn't speak at all. Instead, she makes music and sounds. Her best friend, Violet, always seems to know what she's saying.

BLOOMERS

Lilly (aka Silly Lilly)

If there is an adventure to be had, Lilly's at the lead. She's quirky, adorable, FUN, and funny.

Rosey Posey

Rosey loves to laugh, and best of all she can laugh at herself. Rosey also loves to help the other Bloomers look their best. She loves giving others makeovers with honey masks and petal-cures.

Pete Moss

Pete thinks he can conquer any physical challenge: jumping, climbing, lifting, or carrying. Sometimes he finds himself in trouble going too far up or too far out on a limb. That's when he looks to his friends for a helping leaf.

Violet

Violet is a dreamer, and has a unique and brilliant mind. She is an artist and loves painting pictures of how she sees the world: the sky is pink, the garden is orange, and the clouds are beautiful creatures.

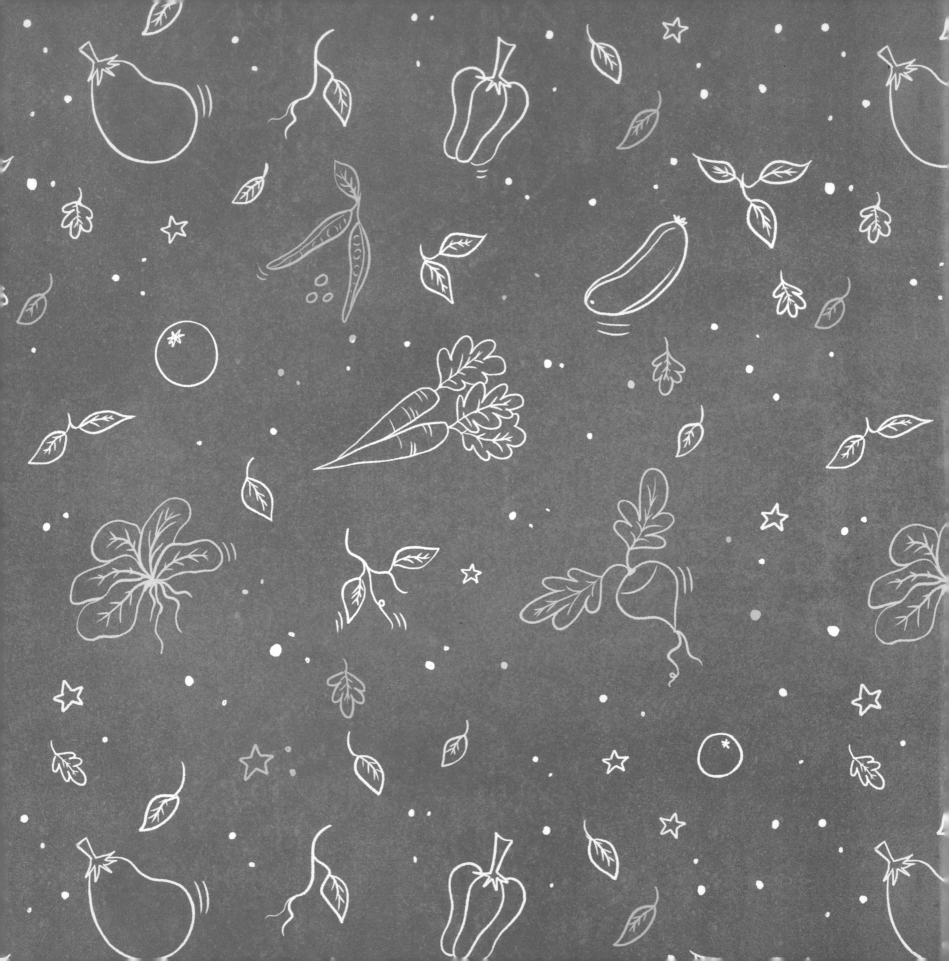